UNICORN RIDERS

We Ride As One

To my children and all those who believe in unicorns — AD
To my children, Clare and Max — JB

Picture Window Books are published by Capstone,
1710 Roe Crest Drive, North Mankato, Minnesota 56003
www.mycapstone.com

Text © 2017 Aleesah Darlison
Illustrations © 2017 Jill Brailsford

Library of Congress Cataloging-in-Publication Data
Names: Darlison, Aleesah, author. | Brailsford, Jill, illustrator.
Title: Quinn's riddles / by Aleesah Darlison ; [Jill Brailsford, illustrator].
Description: North Mankato, Minnesota : Picture Window Books, an imprint of
    Capstone Press, [2017] | Series: Unicorn Riders | Summary: When
    four-year-old Prince Simon is kidnapped the Unicorn Riders are left with a
    trail of taunting riddles which only rider Quinn can solve, and which lead
    them not to the evil Lord Valerian, but to a father and twin sister that
    Quinn never knew she had.
Identifiers: LCCN 2016008011| ISBN 9781479565443 (library binding) |
    ISBN 9781479565528 (paperback) | ISBN 9781479584833 (ebook (pdf))
Subjects: LCSH: Unicorns—Juvenile fiction. | Magic—Juvenile fiction. |
    Kidnapping—Juvenile fiction. | Riddles—Juvenile fiction. |
    Twins—Juvenile fiction. | Sisters—Juvenile fiction. | Adventure stories.
    | CYAC: Unicorns—Fiction. | Magic—Fiction. | Kidnapping—Fiction. |
    Riddles—Fiction. | Twins—Fiction. | Sisters—Fiction. | Adventure and
    adventurers—Fiction. | GSAFD: Adventure fiction.
Classification: LCC PZ7.1.D333 Qu 2017 | DDC 813.6—dc23
LC record available at http://lccn.loc.gov/2016008011

Editor: Nikki Potts
Designer: Bobbie Nuytten
Art Director: Nathan Gassman
Production Specialist: Katy LaVigne
The illustrations in this book were created by Jill Brailsford.

Cover design by Walker Books Australia Pty Ltd
Cover images: Rider, symbol and unicorns © Gillian Brailsford 2011;
lined paper © iStockphoto.com/Imageegaml;
parchment © iStockphoto.com/Peter Zelei

The illustrations for this book were created with black pen,
pencil, and digital media.

Design Element: Shutterstock: Slanapotam

Printed and bound in China.
009694F16

UNICORN RIDERS

Quinn's Riddles

Aleesah Darlison

Illustrations by
Jill Brailsford

PICTURE WINDOW BOOKS
a capstone imprint

Willow & Obecky

Willow's symbol
- a violet—represents being watchful and faithful

Uniform color
- green

Unicorn
- Obecky has a black opal horn.
- She has the gifts of healing and strength.

Ellabeth & Fayza

Ellabeth's symbol
- a hummingbird—represents energy, persistence, and loyalty

Uniform color
- red

Unicorn
- Fayza has an orange topaz horn.
- She has the gift of speed and can also light the dark with her golden magic.

Quinn & Ula

Quinn's symbol
- a butterfly—represents change and lightness

Uniform color
- blue

Unicorn
- Ula has a ruby horn.
- She has the gift of speaking with Quinn using mind-messages.
- She can also sense danger.

Krystal & Estrella

Krystal's symbol
- a diamond—represents perfection, wisdom, and beauty

Uniform color
- purple

Unicorn
- Estrella has a pearl horn.
- She has the gift of enchantment.

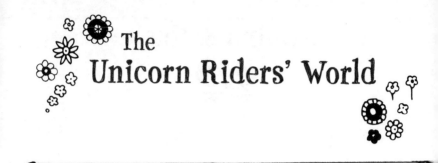

The Unicorn Riders' World

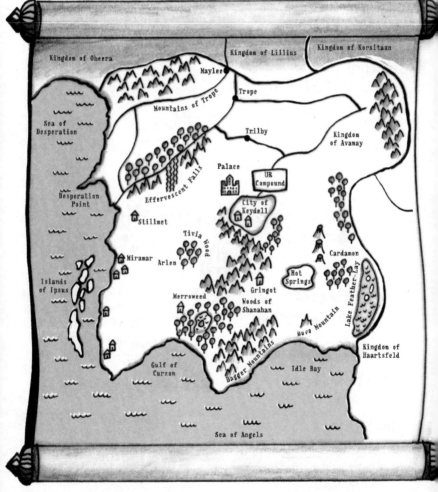

The Unicorn Riders of Avamay

Under the guidance of their leader, Jala, the Unicorn Riders and their magical unicorns protect the Kingdom of Avamay from the threats of evil Lord Valerian.

Decades ago, Lord Valerian forcefully took over the neighboring kingdom of Obeera. He began capturing every magical creature across the eight kingdoms. Luckily, King Perry saved four of Avamay's unicorns. He asked the unicorns to help protect Avamay. And that's when ordinary girls were chosen to be the first Unicorn Riders.

A Rider is chosen when her name and likeness appear in The Choosing Book, which is guarded by Jala. It holds the details of all the past, present, and future Riders. No one can see who the future Riders will be until it is time for a new Rider to be chosen. Only then will The Choosing Book display her details.

• CHAPTER 1 •

QUINN OFFERED A GREEN apple to her unicorn, Ula. "There you go, my beauty. You deserve it," she said.

Ula plucked the apple from her Rider's hand, crunching on it happily. Juice dribbled down the mare's chin and onto the long grass beneath her.

Like all unicorns, Ula had magical powers. One of her unique skills was being able to send mind-messages to her Rider. Gently, she placed the words *Thank you* in Quinn's mind.

"That's my messy girl," Quinn said as she scratched Ula's silky forehead at the base of her spiraled ruby horn.

Quinn was thrilled with Ula today. They had been the best performers during the morning's

9

trick-riding lessons. Trick riding, or mounted gymnastics as Jala, the Unicorn Riders' leader, called it, was an important part of being a Unicorn Rider. The stunts, which came in handy during their adventures, required perfect balance, cooperation, and trust between unicorn and Rider.

Today was the first time Quinn and Ula had won the trick-riding competition, so it was a special day. It meant their skills were improving. And it was a good excuse for a treat.

"Quinn, come quickly!" called Krystal as she came sprinting up.

Like Quinn, Krystal wore a Rider's uniform. But while Quinn's uniform was pale blue with the symbol of a butterfly embroidered on the front, Krystal's was purple with a sparkling diamond.

Jala took great care in selecting each girl's symbol when they arrived at Keydell. A Rider's symbol reflected her personality, so it had to be just right. Quinn's butterfly represented change and lightness. Krystal's diamond stood for perfection, wisdom, and beauty.

"What's happening?" Quinn asked as Krystal danced impatiently from one foot to the other.

"There's a message from the palace," Krystal said. "Jala wants everyone in the meeting room immediately." She rushed off.

Quinn wondered what the message could be.

She gave Ula a final pat, then hurried past the stables, across the courtyard where the Riders and their unicorns gathered before missions, and into the meeting room.

Jala was there already, pacing the floor. Her shoulders were hunched and her brow puckered with worry. Willow, the Head Rider, sat perched on the desk at the front of the room.

Willow was the most experienced Rider. She was tall and slender, and her hair was cut into a short, sharp bob. Willow's uniform was forest green. Her symbol was a purple violet, which stood for being watchful and faithful.

Quinn guessed that Jala had already told Willow about the mission. Willow was chewing her fingernails. She always did that when she was thinking or when she was worried.

Quinn's stomach tensed. *This must be bad,* she thought.

Jala looked at Quinn with a stern gaze. "Where are the other two?" Jala asked.

Quinn blushed. "I don't know," she said.

She squeezed in among the soft, plump cushions lining the bay window. Sunlight streamed in through the glass, warming her face. Outside she saw Old Elsid, the groundskeeper, watering the roses.

Quick footsteps pattered down the hallway. All eyes turned to the door. Krystal slipped in, looking flustered. Ellabeth sauntered in after her, her long dark hair scrunched up in a messy bun.

Ellabeth wore her red uniform with its symbol of a hummingbird embroidered on the front. Her symbol stood for energy, persistence, and loyalty. Like the hummingbird, Ellabeth was always fluttering about or chattering. She hardly ever sat still or stayed silent.

"What kept you?" Jala demanded.

Krystal clicked her tongue. "Ellabeth was in the pavilion. She didn't hear me calling," said Krystal.

13

"I was practicing my self-defense moves," Ellabeth said, whirring her arms around and striking a pose.

"You should have been doing something useful," Krystal criticized.

"Self-defense is useful. You never know when you might need it," Ellabeth said. "Anyway, what were you doing that was useful? Brushing your hair?"

Quinn rolled her eyes. Krystal and Ellabeth never stopped arguing. Jala held up her hand. "Riders, enough. Sit down. You have a mission," she said.

The atmosphere in the room changed instantly. A ripple of nervous excitement splashed through the girls, and they spoke all at once. It had been weeks since their last adventure, when they had accompanied Queen Heart on a trade mission to Costaneera in the south of Avamay. Every Rider itched to escape the estate. The girls knew their unicorns would be eager for a gallop, too.

"I'm glad you're all so eager," Jala said. "Although I must warn you, this mission is a dangerous and complicated one."

"What is it?" Krystal asked. "Tell us."

"Yes, don't keep us waiting," Ellabeth said. "What's going on?"

"Quiet, Riders!" Willow said shushing them.

The girls fell silent.

"Thank you, Willow," Jala said. "Now, here's the news — Prince Simon has been kidnapped."

• CHAPTER 2 •

"KIDNAPPED!" ELLABETH GASPED. "WHEN?"

Quinn was horrified. "Who would do this?" she asked.

The Riders knew the four-year-old prince well. They met with Queen Heart regularly to talk about important matters. The prince was usually hiding behind Queen Heart's silk skirts, staring out at people with his huge, brown eyes.

"Like it or not, there are terrible people in our world," Jala said. "As much as we love the prince, others wish to profit from his misfortune."

Willow's eyes narrowed. "I bet that awful Lord Valerian is behind this," she said.

The other girls murmured in agreement. Lord Valerian had forcefully taken over the neighboring kingdom of Obeera decades ago. Ever since, he had been causing wars and trouble throughout the eight kingdoms.

Lord Valerian was ambitious, cruel, and power hungry. Twice he had tried to invade Avamay. Twice the Unicorn Riders had put a stop to his plans.

No one knew when he would attack again.

"Yes, Valerian sits like a snake waiting to strike," Jala said. "He may be behind this. We don't know. The prince's kidnappers haven't yet revealed themselves."

"All we know is that the prince was on his way to King Rhett's palace in Lillius to visit his cousins," said Jala. "As you all know, King Rhett is Queen Heart's cousin, and the two royals are very close."

"The kidnapping took place near Effervescent Falls, northwest of here," Jala said as she pointed to the map of Avamay hanging on the wall.

"The prince's caravan was ambushed at dusk, and he was stolen from his carriage," Jala explained. "The guards say the kidnappers were well organized, and they knew precisely what they were after. They took the prince before anyone knew what was happening."

"Oh, poor Prince Simon," Quinn said as she gulped back tears. "He must be terrified."

Quinn knew what it was like to be without a family. She had been left at an orphanage as a baby. For her entire life there, she didn't have a single visitor, until Jala came to tell Quinn she had been chosen as a Rider.

A Rider was chosen when their name and likeness appeared in The Choosing Book, which was guarded by Jala. It held the details of all the past, present, and future Riders, but the future Riders could not be seen yet. Only when it was time for a new Rider to be chosen would The Choosing Book display the details.

The woman at the orphanage had been only too happy to be rid of Quinn, for it meant one less mouth to feed. Though she had been a Unicorn Rider for almost a year now, Quinn hadn't forgotten the loneliness of the orphanage. Nor had she stopped wondering why she had been abandoned as a baby. *Had she done something wrong? Was she unlovable?*

Willow squeezed Quinn's hand. "We'll find him. You'll see," Willow said.

"It won't be easy," Jala warned.

"Why not?" Ellabeth said. "We're Unicorn Riders. We can do anything."

The other girls cheered in agreement.

"So you have been listening during lessons not just daydreaming or talking," said Jala smiling.

Ellabeth fidgeted in her seat. "Yes, well . . ."

"And it's wonderful that you believe in yourselves," Jala continued, "but this is no ordinary mission. These kidnappers are playing a cruel and frustrating game with any would-be rescuers."

"What do you mean?" asked Ellabeth.

"They've sent us a riddle we must solve to discover Prince Simon's location," Jala explained.

"Quinn is good at riddles," Willow said.

Quinn blushed. It was true, but she would never have admitted it. She had always loved reading and playing with words and language. Though the orphanage had little money, the library had always been well-stocked. Quinn had  spent many hours there. Now whenever the girls made up riddles or word games, Quinn was always the one to solve them first.

Jala handed Quinn a scroll of paper. "I was hoping I could rely on you, Quinn. See what you make of this," said Jala.

Quinn took the note and read:

"To find where the young royal is kept,
I bid you, friend, this challenge accept.
Journey swiftly to a thriving place,
before the orb of tomorrow's sky hides its face.

Your first clue lies in the bird's joyous call,
your second in the creature that tends flowers all.
What you seek lies within death's deep resting room,
above which tangled snakes do loom.

Speck-sized pyramid of blue corundum for a key,
your only hope of revealing the path to me.
Four chokers of gold, the price to pay,
to end this regal game we play."

"Any ideas?" Jala asked.

A prickle of unease crept along Quinn's spine. Prince Simon's safety, and possibly his life, depended on her. Was she clever enough to solve the clues?

Quinn cleared her throat. "Well, the first few lines are straightforward, I think," she said. "To find the prince, we must play the bandit's game and travel to a busy place before sunset tomorrow."

"What else?" asked Jala.

"The next line is harder. The bird's joyous call," Quinn said.

"That could mean tweet," Krystal offered.

"No, I bet it's squawk," Ellabeth said.

"Not joyous enough," Quinn said. "What about warble, or chirrup, or trill?"

"Could be any of those," Willow replied.

Quinn moved on to the next part of the riddle. "And the bit about the creature tending flowers. I think that's a butterfly," she said.

"What about a beetle?" Willow suggested.

"Or perhaps a bee?" said Krystal.

Quinn nodded. "Maybe," she said. "What about chirrup and bee. Or —" Quinn clicked her fingers. "I've got it!"

"Well, don't keep us in waiting," Ellabeth replied.

"Trill plus bee equals Trilby. The town is Trilby," said Quinn.

Krystal searched the map. "That's northwest of here, isn't it?" she asked.

Jala nodded. "Go on, Quinn," she said.

"Within death's deep resting room," Quinn read out loud as she stared at the ceiling, thinking. *Where does death rest? In the Underworld? In a grave?*

Quinn frowned. It could be anywhere.

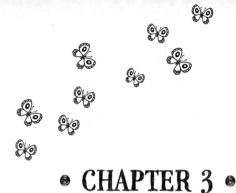

• CHAPTER 3 •

QUINN BEGAN PACING AROUND the room as she read the note again. "Death's deep resting room. If we think about it logically, a room where the dead lie deep might be a grave or underground tomb," Quinn said.

"Which we'd find in a cemetery," said Willow.

Ellabeth shuddered. "Cemeteries give me the creeps," she said.

Krystal shook her head. "Honestly," she said.

"I don't think they mean a grave when they say *room*," Quinn said. "I think it could be a crypt, perhaps. And above the crypt, maybe on the roof or over the door, is some sort of snake pattern."

"And the rest?" Jala asked.

27

"I'm getting to that," Quinn said as she continued pacing. "Speck-sized pyramid of blue corundum . . . Ula's horn is ruby, which I know is red corundum. So then blue corundum must be sapphire. And speck . . ." Quinn paused. She had heard of a speck before, but couldn't remember where. She tugged her strawberry-colored ringlets, trying to think. "Speck. Speck. Oh, I remember!" she exclaimed. "It's an ancient coin, isn't it? We learned about it in our history lessons."

"Well done, Quinn. It is," Jala said. "What about the rest? Can you figure it out?"

Quinn grinned at Jala's praise. "So we use a pyramid-shaped sapphire the size of an old coin as a key," explained Quinn. The pieces of the puzzle slid together in Quinn's mind as she spoke. "And if we do that, we find out where the prince and the kidnappers are. All we have to do is pay four chokers, better known as four hundredweight, of gold, and he'll be ours."

"If you're wrong," Krystal said, "this will cost us valuable time and perhaps the prince's freedom."

"Quinn won't be wrong," Willow said confidently.

Quinn shot Willow a grateful smile.

"I agree," Jala said. "Quinn knows her riddles. Now, go pack your things while I collect the sapphire and gold from the Jewel Room."

The Unicorn Riders were responsible for keeping the royal collection of gems and gold safe. Over five hundred varieties of priceless metals and jewels from across the lands, all carefully collected over the centuries, were kept in the Jewel Room. All the girls loved going in there.

"Oh, can I come?" Krystal pleaded.

"Hey, you went last time," Ellabeth protested.

"No one is going to the Jewel Room," Jala said sternly. "You all need to get ready. You'll be leaving immediately."

Ellabeth rubbed her stomach. "What about dinner? I'm starving," she said.

"How on earth can you be hungry? You've done nothing but play in the pavilion all day," Krystal said.

"I did work," Ellabeth said. "I helped Old Elsid weed the potatoes, and I've got the blisters to prove it." She held up her hands.

"My ointment will fix that," Jala said. "I'll give you some before you leave."

Ellabeth nodded. Jala's magic ointment healed cuts quickly. It was made from a secret recipe passed from leader to leader. Rumor had it that the ingredients used to make the ointment grew beside a hidden spring in the Rider's estate — a spring only Jala knew the location of.

"There's no time for dinner if you're supposed be in Trilby tomorrow afternoon," Jala said as she strode toward the door. "Alda will prepare supplies for your journey. You can eat on the road. Now, go collect your things."

It was nearing sunset when the girls assembled in the courtyard. They each carried a leather pack containing clothes, food, and a portion of gold coins for the ransom. The unicorns pranced about, sensing an adventure. They wore neither bridle nor saddle. It was against the Riders' Code to restrain their unicorns, for they couldn't bear the touch of a bridle around their majestic heads or the weight of a saddle on their proud backs.

The Riders mounted their unicorns — Willow on gentle Obecky, Ellabeth on fast Fayza, and Krystal on dainty Estrella. Lastly, Quinn, the newest and

smallest Rider, mounted Ula by clutching a swatch of her mane and swinging nimbly onto her back.

Jala looked up at the girls. Even in the dim light, her concern was clear.

"Don't worry," Willow said. "We'll rescue the prince."

"It's not just that. I worry about you girls, too," Jala said.

"We'll be back before you know it," Quinn said trying to sound convincing. But she couldn't help feeling a nagging doubt about the mission. So much was riding on her having solved the riddle correctly.

Jala patted Ula's neck. "I hope so," she said smiling.

"Do we ride as one?" Willow shouted.

The Riders answered in unison, their voices echoing. "We ride as one!" they cried.

Then they were off, out through the gates and into the night.

• CHAPTER 4 •

AS HEAD RIDER, WILLOW usually led the way on Obecky. But as the Riders had to gallop quickly through the dark of night, Willow let Ellabeth lead on Fayza, the fastest unicorn. As they set out, magic whirled from the mare's horn. It filled the night with a honey-gold glow, lighting the way and ensuring the unicorns kept up their speed and strength.

When daylight broke, Willow took the lead, although Fayza's magic still kept the unicorns galloping without tiring. By late afternoon, they had reached Trilby. It would have taken a horse much longer to travel the distance. Fayza's magic had saved them valuable time.

Trilby was a large town, bustling with life. The noise of street merchants shouting to sell their goods rose from the streets. The sound of children playing echoed through the alleyways. Carts and wagons loaded with produce rumbled through the streets on their way to the dock. The market smelled of roasting meats, hot buttered corn, and salted nuts. The girls' stomachs rumbled with hunger. They dove into their packs and nibbled on snacks of cheese, bread, and juicy peaches, Alda the cook, had packed for them.

People stopped to stare as the Riders trotted past on their elegant unicorns. The Unicorn Riders always caused a stir. There were many tales about the good deeds they carried out for the queen and how they protected the people from dark forces like Lord Valerian, who threatened the balance of peace and nature.

Not only were the Riders respected for their good deeds, the unicorns were an amazing sight to behold. Their rich, silky coats, flowing manes and tails, and jeweled horns that glistened in the sunlight, struck awe and wonder into all who saw them.

As the Trilbians gathered in the streets to watch the Riders saunter past them, Estrella, Krystal's unicorn, sent sparks of magic from her pearl horn. The sparks settled on the crowd, enchanting and charming them. Krystal put on a good show, too, flicking her long, sun-colored hair and waving and smiling.

She prances about more than Estrella! Quinn thought as she laughed to herself. She watched Krystal accept a bouquet of carnations with all the grace of a queen.

The Riders made their way to the hilltop cemetery. It was a huge place, open to the wind and the sun. The fence skirting the cemetery was made of stones piled waist-high and was covered in lime-colored moss and pale lichen. Ancient magnolia trees, their purple flowers giving off a sweet scent, dotted the grounds. The grass was thick, emerald green, and neatly clipped. Headstones, some new, some weathered by centuries of wind and rain, were organized in line after line of neat rows.

The place was eerily deserted.

"Keep watch, girl," Quinn told Ula as she and the other Riders left the unicorns near the cemetery gates.

Ula could sense danger before others. If anyone suspicious showed up, Quinn knew Ula would tell her.

Quinn stepped cautiously into the cemetery, her pulse thudding hotly in her neck. If she had solved the riddle correctly, the prince and the kidnappers should be here.

Will they play fair? Quinn wondered.

The Riders spread out, stepping carefully between the headstones. Quinn could see and feel the tension in the others. Krystal remained steady, ready for an attack. Ellabeth's face wore the fierce look of concentration she got during self-defense classes. Willow's eyes darted left and right, picking up every tiny movement, her ears pricking at every sound that carried on the breeze.

Then Quinn saw it.

"There," said Quinn pointing to a short gray building huddled among the headstones. Above the doorway, a nest of twisting snakes was carved into the stone. "I think that's it."

Willow nodded. "Krystal, do you have the key?" she asked.

Krystal carefully ripped open the hem of her uniform where she had hidden the jewel for safekeeping. She searched for a place to put the sapphire.

Willow looked at Quinn. "Do you have any ideas?" she asked.

Quinn's heart skipped a beat. *Was she wrong about the riddle?* she wondered.

Quinn ran her hands across the rough stone door, desperately seeking a latch or some other way to open it. Nothing. Stepping back, she gazed up at the twisting snakes. Something wasn't right.

"Pass me the sapphire," Quinn told Krystal. "And I'll need a leg-up."

She placed her boot in the foothold Ellabeth made by locking her hands together. Reaching up, she eased the sapphire into the empty eye socket of the largest snake above the doorway, wriggling it until it fit snugly. A click sounded below.

Krystal looked surprised. "Wow. I think you've got it," she said.

Quinn grinned at Krystal as she jumped down. She pushed against the door. "Need . . . some . . . help," said Quinn.

The other Riders jammed their shoulders against the door and shoved. Stone ground against stone. Slowly, the door slid open.

Quinn held her breath as she peered into the crypt's dim interior.

What would they find inside? Prince Simon? A trap? Nothing?

Cobwebs trailed in tangled threads from ceiling to floor. Stone steps led down into the eerie darkness.

"This place is spooky," Krystal said, her voice echoing around the musty room.

"Calm down," Willow said. "You'll scare the mouse."

"I'm fine," Quinn said.

Willow laughed. "Not you. Her," said Willow as she nodded toward Ellabeth, who stood pale and quivering nearby.

"So what if cemeteries give me the creeps? Nobody's perfect," Ellabeth snapped.

"So, um, what exactly are we looking for?" Krystal asked.

"Not sure," Willow said. "Maybe we should go in."

Ellabeth shook her head. "Forget it," she said. "I'm not going. Uh-uh."

No one else moved.

Quinn sighed. "I'll go," she said.

• CHAPTER 5 •

QUINN CREPT INTO THE crypt, her frightened breathing echoing in her ears. Her nose tingled with the stench of rat droppings, and her throat tickled from the dust. Swiping her hand in front of her, she cleared the sticky cobwebs and peered through the darkness. *Surely they wouldn't keep the prince in here?* she thought.

Quinn came to a room where shelves of dust-covered coffins lined the walls. Something caught her eye: a roll of yellow paper tied with a purple ribbon. Unlike the coffins, it had no layer of dust. It must have been put there recently.

Quinn snatched the paper and ran out of the crypt. "I found something," she said.

"Please, don't be another riddle," Krystal said.

"Yeah, riddles hurt my head," Ellabeth moaned.

Quinn unraveled the paper. "Prepare yourself for a headache, then, because it's a riddle," she said.

She began reading.

"Pomp and grandeur on a royal scale,
now lies lost in all but ancient tales.
Held aloft like the eagle's flight,
can you guess this place of bygone might?

If you do, then travel there swift,
bringing with you the requested gift.
You'll discover the next clue in this game,
and the princely prize, have a chance to reclaim."

Krystal turned to Quinn. "I thought you said Prince Simon would be here?" said Krystal.

Willow placed a hand on Krystal's shoulder. "Calm down, K," she said. "Quinn just deciphers the clues, she doesn't make them up. Whatever game the kidnappers are playing clearly isn't over."

"I'm sorry," Krystal said, kicking at a loose stone with her boot. "I just don't understand why they don't tell us where they are so we can give them the ransom money."

"And so we can get the prince back," Ellabeth said.

Willow shrugged. "Perhaps they're trying to buy themselves time," she said. "Perhaps they enjoy making us squirm." She turned to Quinn. "Do you think you can solve this latest one?" she asked.

Quinn sat down to think. So much was at stake. *What if she couldn't solve the riddle? What would happen to the prince?* she wondered.

A familiar whinny made Quinn look up. Ula was watching her from the other side of the cemetery fence. A magical spark of understanding jumped between Ula and Quinn.

Believe in yourself, Ula said. *You can do this.*

Quinn wasn't so sure.

She rose and wandered away from the others, studying the township below. Smoke rose from chimneys as the afternoon shadows lengthened and the air cooled.

"Pomp and grandeur on a royal scale, now lies lost in all but ancient tales," Quinn said as she racked her brain, thinking of the history lessons Jala had taught them. Throughout the eight kingdoms, there existed many sites where castles had once stood.

Did the riddle mean in Avamay, or somewhere else? Quinn wondered.

Quinn watched the other Riders, heads bent together. *Were they talking about her?* She ducked her head to read the riddle again. "Held aloft like the eagle's flight," she read.

It must be somewhere high, she thought.

Something Jala had said during their lessons came galloping back to her.

"I think I've got it!" she said waving the paper like a flag. The other Riders ran over.

"Well?" Willow said.

"Pomp and grandeur on a royal scale that's now lost," Quinn began, "and it's held high like an eagle flies. I'm guessing it has to be in the mountains. It's a place where a great castle once stood. And where kings and queens ruled. I think it's Maylee."

Krystal frowned and stuck her hands on her hips. "It could be any number of places, Quinn. Are you sure?" she asked.

"Sure as I can be. I'm afraid I have bad news, too," she said. "The second part of the riddle says we'll find our next clue there and have a chance to reclaim Prince Simon."

"And?" Willow said.

"It means even when we reach Maylee, we only have a chance to get him back," said Quinn. "He may not even be there. Nothing is certain."

"What if this is a trap?" Ellabeth said.

"It probably is a trap," Krystal said. "The riddles are just a game designed to lead us into the kidnappers' clutches. Maylee is deep in the Mountains of Trope. Right near Obeera and Lord Valerian. The whole region is dangerous because of that alone. Never mind the treacherous roads or the awful weather."

"It's a huge risk we'll be taking," Quinn said. "But all I know is what the clues are telling me. Like I said, nothing is certain. We could still fail this mission."

"Queen Heart will never forgive us if we do," Krystal said.

"Neither will we," Quinn said.

"We can't afford to think about failure," Willow said. "We're Unicorn Riders. We can do anything. Right, Ellabeth?"

Ellabeth caught onto Willow's enthusiasm. "Right. We ride as one!" she said, her voice echoing around the lonely cemetery, making everyone jump.

"We ride as one," Willow repeated. "Krystal, bring the sapphire. Let's go, Riders."

"Don't need to tell me twice," Ellabeth said as she glanced over her shoulder. "It's getting dark, and this place is scary."

"*Woo-ooooo,*" Krystal howled like a ghost.

Ellabeth squealed, then promptly whacked her.

• CHAPTER 6 •

THE RIDERS SET OUT again, this time, toward Maylee in the Mountains of Trope. Luckily, they had their coats in their backpacks, for it was bitterly cold in the mountains, even in springtime. The wind howled around them, and swirling black clouds threatened rain as they rode deeper into the mountains.

The Mountains of Trope were row after row of dark, jagged hills stretching toward Obccra in the North and the Sea of Desperation in the West. The road to Maylee was narrow and overgrown from years of neglect. It snaked along razor-thin ridge tops where the ground dropped away into deep, rocky gorges.

Ula nickered and pawed the ground.

Take care, she whispered in Quinn's mind.

Quinn warned the others. Instantly, they became alert.

Krystal, who had grown up in the lush Lacey Valley, said, "Only a goat would live here. Not enough trees or flowers for my liking." The wind whipped at her hair, and her cheeks were pink from the cold. She looked miserable.

"Or mirrors, I bet," Ellabeth said, teasing Krystal.

"That's just not funny, Ellabeth," Krystal huffed, sticking her nose in the air.

"Ooh, the truth hurts," Ellabeth barked.

Busy teasing Krystal, Ellabeth wasn't watching the path, and she let Fayza trot. It was true that Fayza was the fastest unicorn, but she was not as sure-footed as the others. She sometimes needed careful guiding, especially on decaying mountain trails.

"Look out," said Quinn, watching in horror as the path dropped out from beneath Fayza's hooves.

Ellabeth and Fayza started sliding down the hillside. Fayza was able to stop just before the edge.

Fayza whinnied.

"Help!" Ellabeth cried. "Help!"

Scrambling and sliding, Fayza slipped closer to the edge. Sharp rocks crouched in the gorge below.

"Hold on," Willow said as she urged Obecky down the slippery slope toward Fayza. Great chunks of dirt and rocks gave way beneath her, yet Obecky managed to stay upright.

"Be careful, Willow," Quinn called after her.

"Use your magic, Obecky!" Willow said.

Gray-blue sparks spiraled out of Obecky's black opal horn. They settled on Fayza and Ellabeth, holding them firm and calming them. Obecky backed up the hillside, straining with all her might. At first, nothing happened. Then she slowly drew Fayza and Ellabeth back up the hillside with her, inside the cloud of soothing, protective magic.

Several tense minutes later, Ellabeth and Fayza were safe, back on the mountain path. Obecky shook her head. The sparkling magic disappeared. Fayza snorted, and Ellabeth gave a cry of surprise and relief.

"Are you all right?" Quinn asked.

Ellabeth's face was pale, and her hands shook. "I'm fine," Ellabeth mumbled, leaping off Fayza to check her all over. "But Fayza's bleeding," she said as she pointed to her unicorn's leg.

"Obecky can fix that," Willow said.

Obecky lowered her horn toward Fayza's injured leg. Gray-blue sparks swirled around the wound for a moment.

Fayza nuzzled Obecky, and Ellabeth hugged her neck.

Willow inspected Fayza's leg. "She'll be fine," she said. "It's only a graze. Obecky's magic has cleaned the wound so it will heal. We'd better keep moving. Time is slipping away."

The girls rode on, all of them shaken by Fayza and Ellabeth's brush with danger. No one spoke for a long time.

Eventually, they came to a clearing littered with ruins. The wind dropped, and the sun burst out from behind a cloud, warming everything. The Riders trotted past massive stone columns, some now lying broken and crumbled among the tangled grass. "What was this place?" Ellabeth asked.

Quinn laughed. "Don't you listen to anything Jala tells us in our history lessons?" she joked.

Ellabeth shrugged, still shaken from her accident. "Not really," she replied.

"Not everyone finds history as interesting as you do, Quinn," Willow added. "Why don't you explain to Ellabeth what this place was?"

Quinn was only too happy to oblige. "Maylee used to be Avamay's main trade center," she explained. "They sold everything here, like silk, tea, and spices. Basically, Maylee was a huge hub that linked the four kingdoms of Lillius, Obeera, Korsitaan, and Avamay. The ruins we're passing now would have been the Great Castle where the Thousand Year Kings lived."

"But when Lord Valerian invaded Obeera, he wrecked it all," Quinn went on. "He made the people

fight each other. The ones who stayed were either forced to be slaves or work for Valerian."

"Rather nasty people, you might say," Willow said.

"The kind to kidnap a prince," Krystal added.

Quinn nodded. "Maybe," she said. "Of course, with a neighbor like Valerian, the royal family couldn't stay here anymore. It was too dangerous. So they moved to Keydell and built another palace. That's where they've lived ever since. Earthquakes, caused by Valerian's misuse of magic, helped tear this place down."

"Typical Valerian," Ellabeth growled.

"When all of this chaos was taking place, King Perry, Queen Heart's father, asked the unicorns to help protect Avamay," Quinn explained. "Valerian was capturing every magical creature across the eight kingdoms. He stole sea serpents, griffins, dragons, and everything he could lay his hands on. It was like he wanted to steal all the magic in the world so that only he could control it. And what he couldn't capture, he destroyed. Luckily for us, King Perry saved four of Avamay's unicorns. As far as we know, they're the only ones left."

"And that's when ordinary girls like us were chosen to be the first Riders, wasn't it?" Ellabeth asked.

"Yes," Quinn said. "And since then, there have been many other Riders over the years."

"But only ever four at a time," Willow said. "Unless we find more unicorns or ours have foals, that's how it will stay."

A distant tinkling sound caused the Riders' ears to perk up.

"What's that noise?" Krystal asked.

"Sounds like bells," Willow said. "Stay alert, Riders."

• CHAPTER 7 •

KRYSTAL'S HANDS FLEW UP defensively. Quinn's heart thudded, and she gripped Ula's mane tightly.

What's waiting for us in Maylee? Quinn wondered.

As they rounded the corner, they came upon rows of run-down cottages, shops, and taverns clinging to the steep hillside. Many had their windows boarded up, boards falling loose, and roofs caving in. Weeds and garbage littered the streets. The cobblestones were chipped and in disrepair.

The unicorns' hooves clattered loudly in the silence.

"Careful, Riders," Willow warned. "These loose stones are dangerous."

Ellabeth shuddered. "This place is as scary as the cemetery," she said.

"I agree," Quinn said. "If Prince Simon is here, he must be very scared."

Up ahead, goats wandered the deserted streets. At the sight of the girls and their unicorns, they bleated and trotted away, their bells tinkling as they went.

"I told you only goats would live here," Krystal murmured.

"Not only goats," Willow said. "Someone had to tie those bells on."

Quinn's neck prickled. Something didn't feel right. Ula nickered nervously, picking up on Quinn's tension. Or something else.

"Does anyone else get the feeling we're being watched?" Krystal asked.

Quinn nodded. Ula tossed her mane, seeming to agree.

Willow glanced up the hillside where remains of more buildings perched. "The kidnappers know we're here," she said. "They'd have lookouts for sure, and they'd have seen and heard us long ago."

"What's that?" Quinn asked pointing to a statue of a man with its arms and legs crumbling. Wound around one broken-off arm was a square of cloth with words painted on it in red. Quinn tugged the cloth down.

She held the cloth and read its words.

"Bravo, dear friends, for making it to Maylee.
Now your task is to seek a certain key.
Amidst bleating companions it does dangle,
on occasion you may hear it jangle.

'Tis the way to reveal the secret within,
the place labeled a kind man's inn.
Now time runs short, don't delay,
our game must end this very day.

To make this sport fun for all,
you'll race against the style's fall.
Ten less six the stroke to beat,
upon the dish that feels Sol's heat."

Still holding the square of cloth, Quinn slid off
Ula. She scratched the unicorn's forehead as she tried

to decode the riddle. When a baby goat trotted by, bleating for its mother, Ula nudged Quinn.

"No more apples," Quinn said. "Nibble some grass if you're hungry."

An image of a goat popped into Quinn's mind.

Quinn's eyes lit up with realization. "Why, Ula, you are clever," she said.

The mare tossed her mane in agreement.

"Have you worked it out?" asked Willow.

"No," Quinn said smiling. "But Ula has. The riddle says we have to find a key that is tied around the neck of an animal that bleats. Now, if Ula isn't mistaken, the bleating animal is a goat. So

the key dangles, like the clapper inside a bell on one of the goats."

"This is impossible," Krystal said, throwing her hands in the air. "How are we ever going to catch all those smelly goats, *and* check all of their bells keys?"

"Even if it is impossible," Willow said, "we must try our best for Prince Simon."

"I know. You're right," Krystal said nodding. Ellabeth turned to Quinn. "What about the rest of the riddle, then?" she asked. "Can you tell us what it means?"

Quinn frowned, thinking for a moment before speaking again. "The second part of the riddle says we use the key to unlock the door of a kind man's inn," she said. "I'm sure it'll make sense when we find it."

"There's more, isn't there?" Ellabeth asked as she snatched the cloth from Quinn. "What does this mean? The bit about racing against the style's fall?"

"If you'd give it back to me I could work it out," Quinn said.

"Calm down," Ellabeth huffed, handing over the cloth.

Quinn re-read the riddle. *Style's fall. Style's fall.* "When I was at the orphanage, we had a sundial built," she said.

"And what does that have to do with anything?" Ellabeth asked.

"Well, we didn't get a lot of visitors in the orphanage, so it was always a treat to speak to outsiders," she said. "I think I must have asked them a million questions about that sundial!" Quinn laughed, remembering. "They ended up telling me all about sundials, you know, explaining all the different parts of them."

"And the point is?" Ellabeth said.

"Well, that is exactly the point!" Quinn said laughing again. "A style is the *pointer* on a sundial. You see? The riddle is telling us we have to race against time. Ten less six is —"

"Four!" Ellabeth shouted.

"Four," Quinn said at the same time. "So we have to get to the inn by four."

Willow looked at Quinn. "You've been right on everything so far," she said. "As I knew you would be. I know you're right on this, too."

Krystal nodded. "I agree," she said. "You've proven you know more about riddles and the meaning of words than all of us put together. I'm sorry I doubted you before."

Quinn saw Ellabeth nodding, too, and she couldn't help smiling. "Thanks," she said.

"What time is it now?" Krystal asked Willow.

Willow opened her ringdial, a miniature version of a sundial. She turned it north and watched where the sun's rays fell. "It's three o'clock," she said.

"That gives us only one hour," Quinn said as her stomach knotted with tension.

• CHAPTER 8 •

ELLABETH GASPED. "ONE HOUR? That's not nearly enough time," she said.

Willow folded her ringdial shut with a click. She slipped it back into her pocket. "It's going to have to be. Now, let's go catch those goats," Willow said.

"Do we have to?" Krystal asked as she wrinkled her nose. "They smell so awful."

Ellabeth laughed. "Huh! I thought that was your perfume," she teased.

"That's not funny, Ellabeth," Krystal sniffed as she flicked her hair.

"Enough, you two," Willow said. "Come on. We'll chase them up that alleyway and then check their bells."

The Riders spread out around the animals to herd them up the street, but the goats scattered in every direction.

"Stop them!" Willow cried. "We can't afford to let them get away! The prince is depending on us."

Grumbling under her breath, Krystal dashed down the alleyway after several escapees.

"Guess we won't be seeing her for awhile," Ellabeth groaned.

"It's up to us three then," Quinn said. "Come on. Remember we're doing this for Prince Simon."

The girls continued to herd the goats without much success.

Krystal then reappeared, waving a handful of green weeds in front of the goats as they trotted eagerly after her.

"Brilliant idea, Krystal," Willow said.

Quinn and Willow plucked handfuls of weeds from an overgrown garden nearby. While they tempted the goats with the food, Krystal and

Ellabeth shooed them from behind. Soon, all the animals were cornered at the end of the alleyway.

"Now for the key," Quinn said as she waded through the bleating animals. The other Riders followed. One after the other, they checked their bells. "Nothing. Nothing. Still nothing . . ." said Quinn.

"Krystal was right — these goats do smell," Ellabeth said as she pinched her nose.

Krystal looked stunned. "So for once you agree with me?" she asked.

"I suppose," Ellabeth huffed. "Boy, this is taking forever."

"Just keep checking," Quinn said. "It has to be here somewhere."

"Quinn's right," Willow said. "Come on, Riders, we need to work together."

Quinn bent to check the bell on the next goat. There weren't many left.

Please be here. Please be here, she prayed.

Quinn's fingers felt something hard and bumpy. *Could it be?*

Quinn grabbed a silver key from the bell. She held it up and smiled. "This has to be it," she said.

Ellabeth squealed and hugged Quinn. "You found it," said Ellabeth. "Awesome! Now let's find that kind man's inn."

"How much time have we got?" Quinn asked.

Willow checked her ringdial. "Seven minutes," she said.

"Hurry! We're running out of time!" Quinn exclaimed.

The Riders quickly hid the gold they had brought in some nearby cottages. Then, leaving the unicorns near the crumbling statue, the girls raced through the streets with the key. They scanned broken signs hanging above doorways and in the windows.

Tailor. Butcher. Crow Foot Tavern. They passed sign after sign. *Baker. Tallow Maker. Polly's Shoes and Shine.*

"This is worse than trying to find a needle in a haystack," Ellabeth moaned.

"Or a key among a thousand goats," Krystal said.

"What I'd like to know is why the kidnappers don't just swap the prince for the gold and let him go," Quinn said.

Willow shrugged. "Maybe this game is about more than just the gold," she said.

"Shame on them for using Prince Simon like this," Krystal said. "Queen Heart must be so worried."

"Any mother would be," Willow said.

Quinn kicked a cobblestone. "Not mine," she said.

"Sorry, Quinn," Willow said gently.

"It's not your fault," Quinn said as she flashed Willow a hollow smile as they walked. "Anyway, it wasn't so bad at the orphanage. And now —"

"Now you've got us," said Willow.

"Yes," replied Quinn.

Quinn knew Willow's words were meant to comfort her, but her heart still ached.

Memories of Quinn's lonely childhood suddenly began playing over in her mind. She had pushed them away for so long, but now they came flooding back to her. She shivered. She didn't need anyone. She learned that early on. She stood alone.

Ellabeth peered up at the rooftops. "Did you hear that?" she asked.

"We are definitely being watched," Krystal said.

Quinn's neck prickled again. "I think you're right," she agreed.

"Which means the kidnappers *are* here," Willow said looking around. "Is Ula telling you anything?"

Quinn listened for a moment. "No," Quinn replied.

Willow checked her ringdial. "We've hardly any time left," she gasped. "Where is this place?"

They ran down another cobblestone street.

"This looks like an inn," Quinn said as she halted outside a stone building with boarded-up windows. The door was thick oak, scarred, and blackened with age, but still solid. A rotting timber sign lay on the ground in front of the building. Quinn flipped it over and saw the faded image of a kind man's face.

"This must be Good Fellows Inn," Quinn said looking at the man's face. "Good fellow. Kind man. I wonder if this is it?"

"Only one way to find out," Ellabeth said as she pushed past Quinn. She rattled the door handle frantically. "It's locked."

"Perhaps we need this," Quinn said as she held up the key.

"Wait," Willow said as she held Quinn's arm. "We have no idea what's waiting for us inside."

"Then let me go first," Quinn said. "I get the feeling that it has to be me anyway. I don't know why, I just do."

"Let me come, too," Willow said.

"No. If it's a trap, it's best if only one of us goes," Quinn said. "We don't all want to get caught."

Willow stepped back. "Okay, but if you're not out in five minutes, we're coming in," she said.

"Hurry!" Krystal said. "We're running out of time."

Quinn slid the key into the lock and turned it. The heavy door creaked open. She stepped inside. The door banged shut behind her. Still panting from her race through the streets, Quinn stood for a moment, wondering what to do.

Then everything went black.

• CHAPTER 9 •

SOMETHING MADE OF ROUGH, heavy cloth and smelling of onions had been slipped over Quinn's head and body. Through the material, she heard muffled voices and movements. She felt several pairs of hands grab her.

"Let me go!" Quinn yelled, wriggling and kicking.

A gruff voice, hot against her ear, grunted, "Hold still. I'm not gonna hurt ya."

Quinn yelled and wriggled all the more.

The voice cursed. "Be still," it said.

Tired and short of air and options, Quinn stopped struggling. She was dragged across the floor, then down some stairs. Voices whispered around her. Footsteps shuffled around. She smelled the remains of a fire, heard a door creak open then close with a soft click.

The bag was tugged from Quinn's head. Her eyes slowly focused in the dim light cast by two stumpy candles on a table nearby.

Quinn realized she was in the cellar beneath the inn. Five or six children, about the same age as Quinn, stood in one corner. They were a ragged bunch, all skin and bones, and wearing filthy, ill-fitting clothes. Some had matted hair. Others had no shoes. But the way they held themselves, the anger burning in their eyes, and the sharp jut of their chins told Quinn they were proud and defiant despite their poverty.

Who are they? Quinn wondered. *And why isn't Ula talking to me?*

A collective gasp came from the children. They stared at her as if they had seen a river spirit or a night monster.

"You!" They pointed at her. "You!"

"Quiet," a steely voice ordered from the shadows before a slender figure stepped forward.

Quinn blinked, wondering if her eyes were tricking her. "What?" she said.

The girl who stepped out of the shadows studied Quinn closely before she shook her head. "I don't believe it. How is this possible?" the girl said.

The girl wore pants and a tattered red shirt. A thick braided belt was tied tight around her waist. A bow and a quiver of arrows were slung over her back. Her hair was red like Quinn's, and her eyes were the same shape and cobalt color. The only difference was that the girl had freckles where Quinn did not.

The girl was identical to Quinn.

The girls stared at one another. Eyes burning with wonder, they held their palms out toward each other, as if drawn by magnets. Just as their hands would have touched, the girl ripped hers away from Quinn's.

"I'm the same as you," Quinn breathed, letting her hand drop to her side.

"No!" the girl spat. "You're nothing like me."

A thousand questions flashed through Quinn's mind. One made it to her lips. "Who am I?" she asked.

A man with a red beard and red hair limped forward, leaning heavily on a stick. He was the only adult in the group. "You are the Unwanted," he said.

"Father!" the girl snapped. "I'll handle this."

Nodding and muttering, the man limped back to the children.

"I am Maram Brash, and we are birth twins. Father told me about you," the girl said as she nodded toward the man. "You're bad luck, that's what you are. You're not normal. You should never have lived."

Quinn's mind spun. *She had a father and a sister? Only they didn't want her.*

"Why?" Quinn asked.

"Surely you can see for yourself," said Maram. "You are unnatural. No two people should be identical. Each must be the owner of their own soul. Our mother had to dispose of one of us, so she chose you, the weakling. Someone obviously pitied you and took you in, but to this family you are long dead."

Every word Maram spoke sliced through Quinn's heart. *Was this the truth of her heritage? How could they think this way? It was wrong. Savage.*

I'm not the one who isn't normal. They are, Quinn thought.

Close to tears, Quinn forced herself to stay strong. "Where is our mother?" she asked.

"Dead," the man who was Quinn's father said.

Quinn studied him with eager eyes. He offered her nothing. Neither a flicker of caring or interest.

"The last long winter saw to that," Quinn's father said. "It took most of our people." He shook his head. "The hunger either killed them or drove them off. Shame on them, leaving their little ones to starve."

Quinn flinched. *Isn't that what you did to me?* she thought.

"Thanks to my plan, that's all about to change," Maram said as her lip curled. "As you will soon see. Did you bring the gold?"

Quinn nodded, wondering what had happened to Maram to make her so ruthless. All the years of not knowing her family suddenly seemed better than knowing this.

I really do stand alone, Quinn realized. That's okay. I don't need anyone, but I do need to save the prince.

• CHAPTER 10 •

"WELL, WHERE IS IT?" Maram demanded.

"You'll see the gold when I see Prince Simon," Quinn said, more calmly than she felt.

"I call the shots here, weakling!" Maram said as she pounced on Quinn, twisting her arm sharply behind her back.

Quinn felt the strength in her twin's hold. She was strong, too. Her training had seen to that. But now wasn't the time to show that strength. Not when she was so outnumbered.

Quinn relaxed and let her head droop. "Please," she said. Her voice was weak. "Don't hurt me."

Maram smiled against Quinn's ear. "Out," she said as she drove Quinn up the stairs.

"Did our father put you up to this?" Quinn asked.

"He's *my* father," Maram seethed. "Not yours. Weren't you listening?"

"I'm sorry," Quinn whimpered. "It's just, you've got it all wrong. Twins aren't bad luck."

Maram twisted Quinn's arm harder behind her back. "Stop talking nonsense," she said. "You don't want to make me angry."

"Of course not. Only, you don't have to do this. You shouldn't let the others make you," Quinn said.

"Them? They're nothing," said Maram. "I'm the leader of this group. I make the decisions."

"How come you're the leader?" Quinn asked.

"Father was our leader until he was injured during a raid last year. Broke his back," she said. "He's only just walking again after I nursed him back to health. As his oldest, *only* child, I was given his position."

"Was it you who decided to kidnap the prince and hold him for ransom?" Quinn asked.

"Yes," Maram said smugly. "As I suspected, it got us far more than gold. I knew the Riders would come, but I didn't know you were one of them. We all thought you were dead. What will your friends think once they discover your family members are criminals?"

Shame flickered in Quinn's brain. *What will the others think of me now? And Jala? Will they abandon me, too? Make me leave Keydell and Ula?*

She couldn't bear to think about it.

"So why all the riddles?" Quinn asked. "Why didn't you just tell us where Prince Simon was in the first place?"

"That wouldn't have been any fun now, would it?" Maram said. "Besides, we needed time to make sure our plans were perfectly in place. To make sure the Riders received the welcome they deserved."

"So you wrote the riddles?" asked Quinn.

"No. That was Father," Maram replied. "He's crazy about riddles, always has been."

Just like Quinn.

By now, they had reached the inn door. One of Maram's group opened it. Maram shoved Quinn outside. The other children followed.

Quinn saw the other Riders surrounded by boys and girls holding clubs and sticks. More of them! They looked fierce and desperate. Just like Maram.

The unicorns had also been captured. They nickered and pawed the ground, thick ropes rubbed against their graceful necks. The pain made them powerless. Quinn almost cried when she saw Ula's head drooping so low her nose touched the ground.

That was why Ula wasn't communicating with her.

She could see the mare's sides heaving with the effort of staying on her feet. She could feel Ula's pain and sensed the terrible ache in her mind.

Quinn sent her a mind-message. *I will save you, Ula. Hold on.*

I'm trying, Ula replied through the pain.

"Quinn!" Willow cried. "You okay?"

"I'm fine. That was a long five minutes, though," Quinn said.

Willow pointed to the ropes binding her wrists. "Yes, well, we're a little tied up here," she replied.

"How come you two look the same?" Ellabeth asked as she gazed at Maram, then Quinn, and then Maram again.

"I'll explain later," Quinn said.

"Enough talk," Maram said. "Where's the gold?"

"I need to see the prince first," Quinn said.

Maram nodded to a boy standing on a balcony across the street. The boy disappeared inside and then returned, dragging the prince with him.

"Prince Simon," Quinn called. "Are you all right?"

The prince's face was dirty, and he had clearly been crying. "I'm a little bit all right," he sniffed. "But I'm a bigger bit not all right. Have you come to take me home?"

Quinn smiled comfortingly. "Yes, we have," she answered. She turned carefully toward Maram, who still held her. "The gold is hidden in one of those houses," Quinn said as she nodded downhill toward a row of battered, orange-roofed cottages. "If you let everyone go, you can have the gold, and I swear we won't follow you."

Quinn saw a message in her mind from Ula. She heard a whisper of the word, *Beware.*

Maram laughed bitterly. "Haven't you guessed?" she said. "We're taking the gold *and* the unicorns. Lord Valerian has offered us a fortune for them. No more hard winters for us."

Quinn struggled against Maram's hold. "I'll die before I let you take them," said Quinn.

Maram twisted Quinn's arm tighter. "As you wish," said Maram.

• CHAPTER 11 •

"NO!" WILLOW CRIED.

Ula whinnied, straining at the ropes binding her. *I'm coming,* she whispered in Quinn's mind.

Quinn realized she had to do something, and fast. Now was the time to use her training and her strength.

Quinn lifted her boot and stomped hard on Maram's foot. At the same time she used her free arm to elbow Maram in the stomach. Bellowing in rage and pain, Maram loosened her grip, allowing Quinn to break free.

"Come back here, weakling, or you will lose your friends and the unicorns!" Maram yelled after Quinn.

Quinn turned to face her twin. From the corner of her eye, she saw Ula's gaze fixed loyally on her. She felt the sun's warmth on her face, and the wind in her hair. She smelled the fresh scent of pine needles, and the feather-light touch of buttercups against her fingers.

You are not alone, Quinn, said Ula. The words swirled in Quinn's mind. *You have me.* Quinn knew Ula was fighting the pain with all her strength.

The mare's magic wove around Quinn, comforting her, protecting her, and making her strong. She felt the strength to forget the pain of loneliness, and to fight her sister.

Maram tossed her bow and arrows to the ground. She lunged forward, her hands outstretched and ready to clutch Quinn's throat.

With a cry of "Kee-ha!" Quinn whacked Maram's hands away. Hard.

Maram screamed, gathering herself up to attack again.

While Quinn and Maram fought, the unicorns sprang to life. Obecky sent her gray-blue protective sparks shooting out of her horn, but her magic was weakened by the ropes. Kicking and rearing, the unicorns whirled around, desperately trying to ignore the pain of the ropes. Even in their weakened

state, their hooves and horns frightened the kidnappers, sending them scattering in all directions.

Krystal got close enough to Estrella so the mare could touch her pearl horn to the ropes binding her wrists. The knots melted away. Krystal untied the other Riders' bindings. Then they tugged the ropes off the unicorns' necks.

As the twins wrestled on the ground, Maram's father yelled, "Get those unicorns! We need them!"

The children darted back in to attack the Riders.

Quinn overcame Maram and sat on top of her, pinning her arms to her sides.

"Get off me!" Maram screamed. "I hate you!"

Quinn stared at her furious twin, thinking it was the strangest thing to see her own face reflected back at her with such hatred. How she would have loved to wipe that look from her twin's face forever.

Filled with rage, Quinn raised her hand to strike Maram. Time froze.

It would be so easy to hurt her now. Hurt her like she's hurt me, she thought. Quinn's hand rose higher. The temptation to hurt Maram grew. But two questions seeped into her mind:

Would it make her feel better? Would it change anything?

Inside herself, Quinn found the answers.

No, it wouldn't. This wasn't what she wanted.

Quinn didn't feel hatred like Maram, and she knew that was a good thing.

"You are *so* not worth it," Quinn said as she rolled off her sister and stood up.

Good girl, she heard Ula whisper in her mind.

Quinn shot Ula a worried look.

I'm fine, Ula sent back to her.

Using Maram's braided belt, Quinn tied her sister to the crumbling statue.

"You are nothing, weakling!" Maram seethed. "You *have* nothing."

"You're wrong," Quinn said. "I have the Riders *and* I have Ula." Then she dashed into the battle.

All four Riders now stood back to back as sticks clubs flew around them. They were surrounded by children and completely outnumbered.

Obecky tried her magic again. It was stronger this time. The other unicorns had recovered slightly, too. Whinnying shrilly, they galloped toward their Riders. Sparks flew and magic whirled as Obecky's protective shield settled around them.

Willow, Ellabeth, and Krystal jumped up onto their unicorns.

Obecky lowered her horn at one of the attackers. Willow seized the boy's club. "That's enough from you," she cried. "Surrender now!"

"Don't hurt me!" he squeaked, bounding away like a rabbit with a fox on its tail.

More kidnappers were scattering, disappearing up the hillside, and slipping away through the buildings and the rubble.

Quinn spotted Prince Simon, still being held on the balcony by a few remaining kidnappers. Forgetting the pain in her arm, she leaped onto Ula's back and galloped toward him. "Prince Simon, jump! I'll catch you!" yelled Quinn.

The brave little prince tore free from the hands that gripped him. He ran to the balcony's ledge. Quinn leaped up and stood on Ula's back. She stretched her arms wide, just like she had done during her trick-riding lessons.

Prince Simon leaped off the

balcony into the air. Quinn held her breath and thought, *please let me catch him!*

Prince Simon landed in Quinn's arms with a thud. She clutched him to her and dropped down onto Ula's back. Quinn galloped toward the other Riders. As she passed the statue, her eyes looked for her sister.

Maram was gone. So were her followers.

"Oh no, they've gotten away," Krystal moaned.

"It'll take forever to search for them through these ruins," Ellabeth added.

Willow nodded. "Who knows what hiding spots they might have?" she said. "It's too dangerous for us to stay any longer. We'll send a search party for them later. For now, our priority is to return Prince Simon home safely. Let's go."

Quinn felt a burst of fire through her shoulder. Reaching up, she found the shaft of an arrow piercing her back. Pain exploded inside her, and she began to feel faint. She turned to see Maram disappearing down an alleyway, her bow and arrows clutched tightly in her hand.

Quinn slumped forward, in danger of losing the prince. Hands gripped her. She glanced up, fearing it was the kidnappers, but it was Krystal and Ellabeth riding beside her, holding her up.

"Don't worry. We've got you, Quinn," Ellabeth said.

"Thanks," Quinn mumbled through her haze of pain. "I thought I was alone."

"Remember, we ride as one?" Krystal said.

"We ride as one," Quinn murmured before blacking out.

• CHAPTER 12 •

QUINN SAT IN THE garden, lying in the sun and twirling a pink-petaled sweet pea between her fingertips. Ula grazed nearby, occasionally nibbling a rosebud or two when she thought no one was looking.

"How's the shoulder?" Jala asked, sitting beside Quinn.

"Better now," Quinn replied. "Thanks to your ointment."

"Amazing stuff," Jala said. She nodded toward the flower in Quinn's hand. "Ah, my favorite."

Quinn dipped her head to take in the flower's scent. "They're my favorite, too," she said.

"What do you like about them?" Jala asked.

"Oh, well, they're delicate and soft and smell amazing," Quinn said. She scrunched her nose. "That sounded silly."

Jala laughed. "Not at all," she said. "I like how they look and smell, also. But more than that, I see the sweet pea standing for something special and unique."

"Which is?" asked Quinn.

"Strength," Jala replied.

Quinn's brow furrowed. "How can something so delicate be strong?" she asked.

"Because the sweet pea grows all through the cold, lonely winter," Jala said stretching her long legs out as she spoke. "Then in spring, with the lightest touch of the sun's warmth, it produces the most delicate, sweetly-scented blossoms. It's a contradiction. Delicate yet strong. Like you."

Quinn's eyebrows jumped. "Like me? How?" she asked.

"Because you're tough. You're a survivor," said Jala. "Yet you're also a kind and sensitive person. All the other Riders admire you."

Embarrassed, Quinn studied her flower.

"And we're all sorry you had to learn the truth about your family the way you did. None of us knew," Jala said.

"It's okay," said Quinn. "I'm happy here."

Jala edged forward in her seat, gazing at Quinn intently. "Are you? Really?" she asked.

"Yes," Quinn replied. Her smile held warmth and truth. "I love it here. I love Ula. I love the other Riders. They're my friends and my family now."

"You aren't alone anymore," said Jala.

Quinn nodded.

"You also know you're nothing like Maram, don't you?" Jala asked.

"I look just like her," Quinn said. "I could have ended up like her." She shook her head. "I knew the search party wouldn't find Maram. She's too clever.

But one day I will find my sister. I feel it in here," she said as she pressed her hand against her heart.

"It doesn't mean you'll be able to save her," Jala said. "Or that she'll want to be saved."

"I'll still try," said Quinn.

Jala chuckled as she stood up. "Of that I'm sure," said Jala. "Now come. It's time to celebrate your bravery and the prince's safe return. Alda has made us a delicious feast of roast duck, cucumber salad, and caramel tarts for dessert."

"Yum, my favorites," Quinn said, licking her lips.

Jala grinned. "Something else we have in common," she said.

Quinn rose and tugged a green apple from her pocket. "I'll be right in," she said. "I just have to do something first."

Ula spotted the apple in Quinn's hand. Tail up and nickering happily, she trotted over to her Rider.

Quinn offered the apple to her unicorn. "There you go, my beauty. You deserve it."

Glossary

ambitious (am-BISH-uhn)—having a desire to achieve a particular goal

contradiction (kahn-truh-DIK-shuhn)—something that is the opposite of what it seems to be

crypt (KRIPT)—a chamber used as a grave

decipher (di-SYE-fur)—to figure out something that is written in code or is hard to understand

heritage (HER-uh-tij)—history and traditions handed down from the past

kidnap (KID-nap)—to capture a person and keep him or her as a prisoner, usually until demands are met

orphanage (OR-fuh-nij)—a place that provides a home for children whose parents have died

persistent (pur-SIS-tuhnt)—continuing to do something in spite of difficulty or obstacles

shame (SHAME)—a feeling of embarrassment

sundial (SUHN-dye-uhl)—an instrument that shows the time with a pointer that casts a shadow on a flat dial similar to the face of a clock

temptation (temp-TAY-shuhn)—something that you want to have or do, although you know you should not

treacherous (TRECH-ur-uhs)—disloyal and not to be trusted

Discussion Questions

1. How did Quinn's trick-riding skills help her in the book?

2. What things from Quinn's past helped her throughout the book?

3. How did Quinn relate to how Prince Simon must have felt when he was kidnapped?

Writing Prompts

1. Do you think Quinn would have turned out like her sister, Maram, if they'd never been separated? Why or why not?

2. One of Quinn's skills is solving riddles. Write about a skill that you have.

3. The Unicorn Riders relied on Quinn to solve the riddles and find Prince Simon. Write about a time when someone relied on you for help.

UNICORN RIDERS

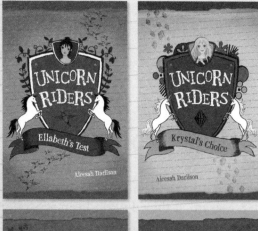

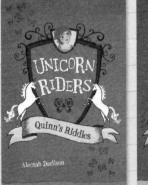

COLLECT THE SERIES!